the Secret Trees

poems

Luci Shaw

Harold Shaw Publishers
Wheaton, Illinois

Acknowledgements

*Grateful acknowledgement
is made to the editors of the
following periodicals, in
which some of these poems
first appeared:*

For The Time Being, HIS,
Interest, The Banner,
Eternity, The Lanthorn,
Christianity Today,
Being Bluebook, The
Christian Reader

Design: Kathy Lay Burrows

*Photo credits:
Cover, Douglas Gilbert
Kathy Lay-Burrows, p. 10;
Rich Ball, pp. 14, 23, 45, 67;
Don Ontiveros, pp. 30, 53, 58
John Shaw, p. 74*

*Library of Congress Catalog
Card Number: 76-1342
ISBN 0-87788-909-0*

*Printed in the United
States of America*

To Tom & Kathy

A Fore Word

If you want to read poetry, and certainly if you want to write it, you have to believe in the Creation. Not just the doctrine of Creation (although one way or another, readers and writers of poetry must have some such notion lurking in their imaginations): you have to believe in the Creation itself, that is, this living, textured, tufted, brindled, knobbly, flowing, turning, pulsating, singing business, this concretion, this pageant, this panoply of antiphons calling back and forth between bright and dim, peak and valley, hot and cold, dry and wet, fortissimo and pianissimo, vast and minuscule, red and blue, lion and lamb, Everest and eidelweiss, archangel and mayfly.

You have to believe in this—that is, you have to believe that it is there, and that it is important. This will appear to be an observation of the most embarrassing banality until we reflect for a minute. Then the bleak truth emerges: most of us live most of the time as though this Creation were unimportant; nay, that it is, in effect, not there.

To be sure, we would reject with some heat the accusation that we let the Creation escape our notice. Why—nobody enjoys a good sunset more than we; and these wonderful maple leaves this October, and the taste of fresh raspberries, and the sheen on the neck of that chestnut gelding, and the feel of grass under our bare feet—who's saying we don't believe in the Creation? We not only believe in it: we love it.

Yes. No doubt we do, from time to time. But that is just the difficulty. It is an intermittent, incidental business with most of us. In so far as we have our attention hailed by some lovely sight or smell or sound, we do feel surging momentarily through us the sap of this Creation. But if we are remorselessly and unsentimentally honest with ourselves, we will have to admit that during the ordinary day and week and month, we pursue our harried way as though the Creation were at best a backdrop, or scrim, for the real activities of existence.

And there is an irony in the situation too. The people who defend the actual doctrine of Creation (that is, orthodox Christians), often end up all unwittingly with an outlook whose net effect is to deny that doctrine. Having as they do a lively awareness of how fleeting this world is, they naturally (and rightly) tend to cast the anchor of their imaginations into the unseen world—the world of "heaven," or "spirituality," or "the eternal." It is meet and right so to do. What is not meet and right to do is to think of that unseen world as the real world, as opposed to this seen, material world which, because it is fleeting, must to that extent be illusory and unimportant. This is Platonism, not to say Gnosticism. It has been rejected as heterodoxy from the beginning by the Church.

To take the Christian doctrine of the Creation seriously is to reject the Gnostic inclination to fly away from the body and from the world of time and sense into a world of pure spirituality. It is to say with God, "It is good," when we look at what He has made. It is to say "Benedicite, omnia opera Domini." It is to mean this, and to live with this on our tongues.

Poets think that the texture and shape and color and taste of things are important, and that the effort to arrest our attention with these textures and shapes and colors and tastes by articulating them in words is a worthwhile effort. Christian poets think this, and more. They think, further, that in thus articulating the world and our experience of it, they are functioning as "makers," made in the image of The Maker and called to exhibit that image by themselves making something. The thing they are making is poetry (the word comes from the Greek verb "to make"). And poetry is by definition a sensuous thing, made of words whose sound hales up all the textures and shapes and colors of the world, and hails our imagination with them.

The poet is obliged to take the Creation and its textures seriously, since it is in the language of those textures that he speaks to us of all the rest of our experience. The delights, perplexities, horrors, and quiet pleasures of life, and the emotions that we feel in response to them, and the mysteries and immensities of the divine Drama—the poet comes at these things, not via abstractions and generalities, but by exact and concrete images which he sees lying all around him all the time.

Luci Shaw shows this. And Luci Shaw writes poetry. Jingle-writers, and doggerel-writers, and verse-writers (what the eighteenth century called "scribblers") are common enough. Poets are as rare as unicorns. Luci Shaw is, I think, a poet. Read her poetry here. Let these verses do what they are made to do—let them delight you and lead you to the regions where you not only reflect on things, but where you grasp and touch and feel them; and where you discover that there is a transubstantiation going on—that what you supposed was "mere" earth bespeaks heaven. This, surely, is at least part of what the Christian doctrine of the Creation is about, and what Christian poetry is about, and what Luci Shaw's poetry is about.

Thomas Howard,
Gordon College

Contents

I
Behind
the
Walls

Behind the walls

Along the street a new house
is going up among the trees.
The open air of Wheaton
is being boxed in there, closed off
from rain, birds, light, leaves.
Day by day another kind of space
is being defined
by upright beams of pine, narrow
yellow in the morning's sun,
sentenced to the long darkness.
Months from now, when it is all done,
I shall walk by. Where others
notice siding, shutters, paint,
I shall see behind the walls
the secret trees
standing straight and strong
as pines in the free groves outside.

Airport waiting room

Nature's wildnesses sprout
in every crowd.
Across the aisle from me
sits a man with a mushroom nose.
My sleeping daughter's ear
is a pale shell delicately
open toward the sea.
My male companion from
Ontario is an oak tree
dropping small truths
like acorns, and from here
I can see shades of windblown hair
diverse as all the
brown prairie grass
of Kansas.

Signs of Spring

The small towns of the midwest! Even
among the green explosions of April
they are quilted to the earth, pinned
at their square corners by the
presidential decorum of Franklin,
Madison, Harrison, Lincoln, Washington
and the systemic botany of Maple,
Elm, Walnut, Oak, Chestnut, Pine or
the pragmatism of First, Second,
Third, Fourth, Fifth and Main.
My mind is bursting with tulips! In a
small rebellion, which has something
to do with the season, my mind frees
from its propriety every street I pass.
Rooting up the iron stalks with their
pale rectangles, here I plant
an oval, there a star, cloud shapes
or small precious circles of violet
and topaz and cerulean blue that say
Peacock Place, Doorway Drive,
Chariot Way, Sing-a-Psalm Street,
Appleseed Avenue, Benevolence Boulevard,
Cranberry Circle, Goosefeather Grange,
Tapestry Turnabout. And, to the
mailman's dismay, I'd refurbish
the landscape and celebrate each spring,
changing the signs again!

To a Christmas two-year-old

Child, and all children,
come and celebrate
the little one who came,
threatened by hate
and Herod's sword.
Sing softly and rejoice
in the reward
for all the baby boys
of Bethlehem
who died
in Jesus' place.

Small wonder when He grew
He wanted children by His side,
stretched out His arms, stood,
beckoned you,
called *Come to me*
and died
in your place
so that you could.

Materfamilias

Mother tree
bald, old
with shoulders
white as
bones bleached
but still green
as a girl
where mosses
crust your south
and life tufts
some of your
knotted fingers
You cup small jays
in your elbows
wrinkle your
brown skin
to shelter larvae
and your roots
beam and buttress
marmot halls

Today
the morning mountain
is a breathless
gold, yet you
bend to an
eternal gale
You are a signal
to weather, a
signpost in time
pointing
the way the wind
went

Fire on the Berkshires, October 1974
Romans 1:20

Across these valleys roared the furnaces
of the Almighty, till all that was left of the leaves
(melted copper and ornamented brass and refined gold)
was a scattered heat that was partly Himself and
partly His sun and partly a glow of my own.

It was snow that slowly extinguished
the blazes of Fall on the flanks of the hills.
But His coals, searing the eyeballs, had kindled
an altar whose fires leap in the brain all this long
winter. They burn and will not be consumed.

The singularity of shells

A shell—how small an empty space,
a folding out of pink and white,
a letting in of spiral light.
How random? and how commonplace?
(A million shells along the beach
are just as fine and full of grace
as this one here within your reach.)

But lift it, hold it to your ear
and listen. Surely you can hear
the swish and sigh of all the grey
and gleaming waters, and the play
of wind with rain and sun, encased
in one small jewel box and placed,
by God and oceans, in your way.

In my living room

I have a carpet, green as outside grass.
Its short, dense, woolly blades all seem to wait
for the old hoover to mow down the dirt
and rake dead fibers, miscellaneous leaves
of lint, into itself. I almost wish
the rain would pour down from the ceilinged sky,
silver and fresh, onto this inside lawn.
Then, from the hanging corner globe, switched on,
(sun breaking through after the shower's over)
a flood of yellow sunlight might bewitch
a robin into pulling at a worm
daring to tunnel the closewoven sod.

The Groundhog

The groundhog is, at best, a simple soul
   without pretension, happy in his hole,
twinkle-eyed, shy, earthy, coarse-coated grey,
   no use at all (except on Groundhog Day).
At Christmas time, a rather doubtful fable
   gives the beast standing room inside the stable
with other simple things, shepherds, and sheep,
   cows, and small winter birds, and on the heap
of warm, sun-sweetened hay, the simplest thing
   of all—a Baby. Can a groundhog sing,
or only grunt his wonder? Could he know
   this new-born Child had planned him, long ago,
for groundhog-hood? Whether true tale or fable,
   I like to think that he *was* in the stable,
part of the Plan, and that He who designed
   all simple wonderers, may have had me in mind.

moonset

thinsilver as
a wish still born
she slides down
sky slopes · sits
on the sea

her mouth is wet
drinking · she slips
under · horizons
drown her bright
forehead

grandmother's
arthritis

after all
her house is
full of useful legs
(chairs tables
beds) that
can't walk
and arms stiff
as boards

Program
for John

The evening trees push into a frozen sky
against the rule of their own iron-dark weight
(a bulk that splinters in its reaching up
though each sharp twig carries a dormant freight
of buds). If you will, you may see a strategy, steady
enough so that spring by spring, when weather is ready
and buds burst, small victories may be won
in the oaks' slow resolute advance upon the sun.
But a snowflake so easily falls *away* from the light
in a chaos of others, letting gravity do the steering.
(The witless suddenness of so much white,
a flurry without effort, overwhelms the clearing,
no tactic needed but the erratic air
to pile snow masses carelessly knee deep.)
Each flake floats, a small silver accident,
to its random place in the drift, and goes to sleep.

You may see no reason, in this winter view,
for keeping on, for persistence, for patient planning.
But soon, with the summer forest warm and glowing
around you, solid, confident, greenly spanning
seasons, and the space between earth and sky,
the flake and the drift and the lunatic whiteness flying
will seem less than memories. You'll know you can reach as high
as a branching tree, maybe higher. You'll keep on trying.

Image

I have written
a finger
and the
delicate bone
of a wrist

perhaps
someday
I will be able
to show you
a torso

Convention

Entombed at night
in the geometric, bright-
ly impersonal room
on the fifteenth floor
under a painting
that knows nothing
of art (better maybe
than the bare wall?)
I stare at the other
rectangle's gray flicker
between the curtained
window and the
repetitious mirror
lying alone
queen-sized and
unhusbanded, nor wakened
by small sleepwalkers.
The bored hum
of the air conditioner
flattens out my nights.
It is a room that by
some cool invisible
magic picks itself up
daily while I'm gone:
the wrinkled bed
resolving itself into
neatness, the furnishings
easing, automatically
into place. Damp towels
vanish, reappear
dry, flat, foursquare.
Breakfast is achieved
at a finger's dial.
It will all be redeemed
by the end of the business,
the plane home, the

explosion of dog and
children at the door;
the roughness of a dozen
reaching arms; a chaos
of clothes in the hamper;
the relief of love renewed;
an almost empty
refrigerator
and nothing automatic
any more.

Rider

There's almost nothing as incongruous
as a very large man laboring
up a hill on a Honda 75.
Unless it is the career of a versifier
inflated with a sense of destiny
urging his miniature talent
up a mountain of immortality.

To K.N.T.

How exciting
to find oneself
in the lion's den
especially since
being there is as
safe as it was
for Daniel
and for the same
reason

Winter wheat

Even the oaks
are almost naked.
The fall flames of rose & gold
have died out under
the dark rains.
The ground underfoot
is rimed with the cold ashes
of the wind, the bleached
stubble, the clotted
weed-heads.

But see,
over there, like a
green wound in the shoulder
of the hill, like a new patch
in the quilt,
blazes a square of quite
improbable emerald.
With what audacity
the bright velvet assaults
our autumn senses:
each blade a reversal
of seasons, its upstart shoot
flagging the brief sun bursts,
the sap juicing to its tip,
ready, now, in November,
for the new year!

The oaks are bare.
The sky is heavy with
first snow. But my rebel blood
beats higher now
against the winter night
coming.

Salutation
(*St. Luke 1:39-45*)

Framed in light,
Mary sings through the doorway.
Elizabeth's six month joy
jumps, a palpable greeting,
a hidden first encounter
between son and Son.

And my heart turns over
when I meet Jesus
in you

To Clyde S. Kilby
on his 70th birthday

It is a time when apples ripen.
friendships thicken,
maples kindle a Fall fire
west of Blanchard. Through the halls
scholars and students quicken
at a familiar voice,
and on the corner of Washington and Jefferson
squirrels and sparrows rejoice
because you're home. Like a hobbit
come back to the Shire
you're home again, our friend,
bringing Martha with you, and sunflower
seeds, a sackful of nuts, three score
years and ten worth of wisdom, under
your arm—letters and Lewis-lore—
your mind a well of wonder.

It was your mind, your inner eye, that
saw it long before it happened—
the hierarchy of shelves
dusted obliquely by the late sun
behind old glass
in the narrow room once occupied
by a minority of one
and now inhabited by Inklings and Elves.
Like a gardener raking grass,
piling the bright and varied leaves,
from far you gathered treasure, sheaves
of manuscripts, papers ornamented
with the rich, crabbed, English script,
searched out the volumes
burnished and precious with
scholarship and age—
"fact shrunk to truth" speaking
from every page.

Then you swung open for us all
the wardrobe door,
pushed us farther up and farther in
(accompanied by some favorite talking beast)
to Middle-earth, Narnia, and the Utter East.
In there, for us to re-explore,
is perfect Perelandra.
Treebeard is growing up the cornered wall.
In the Deep Space behind the rows of books
eldila elude us; Curdie
encounters Mr. Bultitude the bear.
There in that room
we smell the past, untainted by decay or death
but fragrant, for in there
the mallorns bloom
and all the blessed air
is warm with Aslan's breath.

II
Under the Skin

Under the skin

The wind is rising. The golden air
wears at us, lifting the loose hairs
from our heads. Invisible waves
sweep off the grains of skin lying
like sand along the beaches of our backs.

And the sun grinds on,
a hot eye boring into all centers,
vaporizing a hidden pool, shrivelling
initiative, dissolving the wax
of the soul after the body's gone.

An infinite silence whittles away at all sound.
Colors vanish endlessly, like burst bubbles,
like small, innumerable fires gone out
under the round white weight
of a universe too grand for its diversities.

The atmosphere is always at work
polishing at untidiness: all thin
extrusions from the skull of consciousness;
the purple shadows on this planet's chin.
How easily eternity vanquishes the minutes!

Though the burnishing never ends, across
the buffeted skin of earth and man
still sometimes grows a struggling green.
Caught in the gale of space, we may yet discover
what lies behind any individual face.

ascending

for the time
being / the dark earth
was enough
to substantiate you
in our vision

but the universal circle
claimed you / rid
of a finite foothold
you lifted / scattered
your feathers in light
faceted the
invisibilities
of thin air / time & space
after the light-ning
melted in one

blinded / our eyes
turn inward
so we find
your closer paraclete
our truer view

On reading a travel magazine

The phoenix' decorative flames
are about to be extinguished in a
surfeit of holy water. The Ganges
shimmers under my chair
reflecting the convolutions
of the unicorn's unique horn.
Bamboo shoots sprout
like green haiku from the waste
basket. I open my window.
All I can hear is the warm
Tahitian rain.

Poem finding a path

The words stick in the teeth.
Rich and boiling, ideas copulate
with syllables, generate, bubble
inwardly upward, unhindered
until they reach the traffic jam
at the junction of brain, breath, tongue.
There in the gullet they clot, flatten,
turn hard and dull. Wrong pieces
mate and will not come unstuck.
Shards of images, the sentences
stick in the teeth
or issue in an awkward belch,
disturbing the peace

unless they find an alternate
escape route. Somehow the joints
of shoulder, elbow, wrist,
present no obstacle. Along
striated nerves and muscles, the blips
of light and color dance and flow
smoothly, string themselves
on an iambic thread, slip
their enamel down the arm
via ink, assemble, establish
themselves according to their
innate poetry, form rows
and stand up to be read.

eternity seen from North Avenue
November 3

from the top of the
wet road
narrowed by
half a mile
& a steep slope
I see the gray
splay up & over
so that
for an afternoon
all space
is paved with
the same pale rain

there is
no difference
the road has
no end
the horizon
has been abolished
& what
is to stop me
from driving
up the sky?

O'Hareport: Taking off

As the frozen blueprint drops away
below, all sharp gray angles
and etched snow smudged with low fog,
I realize how large a view it is,
and to some degree true: these
spatial relationships are
more precisely drafted than
the landbound ones I am used to.
But the aerial look at an airport
is a geography of the absurd. From this
tilted height the real things are
quite invisible. Feelings, thoughts,
movements are reduced so perilously
small, so infinitely sharp, they are
turned as unreal as atoms. Do the
t.v. antennae, dark bristles on a
cityskin, transmit love or anger?
And the mushroom watertowers—
are they heavy with impatience or
smugness, waiting for the fire?
Does fear rise in the steam
from all those sooted chimneys,
a subtle pollutant? Does death
ride the robot highways? It seems
as if all Chicago may be struggling
to rise from its ice and steel
in a strictly defined chaos
to tell me some urgent reality.
The beginning of the message
buffets me like turbulence just as we lift,
beyond seeing, into the cloud castles.

Shooting gallery

How often
I peppered the walls with prayers
as round & quick
& plastic as the pellets
ready to my trigger, there,
at a dime apiece: aiming
at the painted decoys (each
wooden & safe as a pat answer)
not trying too hard
for fear of
winning
& having to lug
the vulgarity of
a useless prize
under my arm
all the way home.

Still,
it seemed an easier targetry
than shooting at live ducks
with real bullets
until I smelled feathers
& blood.

**"unspeakable the distance
in the mind"**—*Howard Nemerov*

All balled & crossed
& twisted tight
round his cerebral
hemispheres
may be unwound
the crumpled lengths
—his tracks across
the miles, the years.

The tenacity of memory
(*"The vision that the eye accepts outlasts
its object"*)

Even at midnight my lids swarm with the golden bees,
the blues clear as infinity, the greens
whose cool leaves stroke the brain.

The most flagrant of the odors of the sea
are vanished down the wind. I think of ships;
read of Le Havre; my nostrils question the dead air.

Thinking of old winters in Ontario, I shiver.
Childhood's icicles are slipping their shattered
crystal through my mind's fingers.

Though the pomegranate is finished, still
my tongue tingles.
My skull is filled with rubies.

Warm with words, my children's far throats
echo. The shapes of their mouths
kiss every view.

The Joining
—after reading Charles Williams
and Romans 6

After the hours of restless
struggling through the waves
of fears, wounded, stroking against
gravity, treading water, stroking,
I choose to let go, to float
numbed, to trust myself to the words
sung across the lake: *Lay down*
your life, to trust my body to
the drifting wood—in weariness my bed,
my frame, the crux of all matters,
to which he was joined by force
but willingly, laid on it to be
what I have been
to gain my pain
(himself to drown in it).

                      Thus
am I buoyed, and resting there
cruciform, new knowledge laps me
like a wave: *I* am the cross—
coarse grained and pocked with holes
of nails—to which he joins himself
(already joined to his deep baptism)
that he may join me to his strong escape,
his rising from the darkness of
this icy lake.

Botany of a poem

The seed drifts · idea
lights lightly
but decisively on a
head · roots
in cerebral soil
sucks up
such memories as will
nourish
tentative sprouts · gets
green · grows
as light and night
pull it and
let it go · aims its
hybrid flowers
and experimental fruit
in the direction
of some open
ear · finds a crack
and happily drops
a seed in it · takes
root again. . . .

Man cannot name himself

Man cannot
name himself

He waits for God
or Satan
to tell him
who he is

Anatomy of the invisible

What shape is electricity?
What does heat look like if
we have no skin? no eyes?

What stark form rises
in the black framework of
the house of our grief?

How heavy is gravity? with what
implacable patterns does it drag
at us from the earth's core?

Love is a quick rose liquid
or it may curl smokelike
around the tendrils of our minds.

Sound has color, as it pours
into us through our
two funnels of flesh.

Is light granular—a shaft
of sandgold from
beyond us to beyond us?

Or is it a bright wave
that breaks and washes clean
the old world's face?

Fear seems to fall with small
punctiliar precision like
the cold stars of winter.

But blessing comes as a strong
warm wind in the oak trees,
clear, a golden wine flowing.

need is our name

wide is our mouth and
our hands reach always
upward
need is our name

> Giving
> is Yours

we are machines
of no certain function
aching in all our axles
pain is our name

> Healing
> is Yours

we are in battle
between bombs we stumble
over other bodies
defeat is our name

> Triumph
> is Yours

Under glass

hurricane candles
Rhine wine
a seascape (with gulls)
dried grass
three minute's worth
of time
a ship model, ferns
in moss, photographs:
all under glass
(showcases of
ourselves)
wait things to be
seen or saved
or savored
on our shelves

and here
behind the window-
glass of words
the poem on the page
preserves the clear
colors of a vision
displays an etched
view
the clue
to a memory, a green
thought, an intoxicant
idea,
dream wicks
to be lit
also
a portrait of the poet
at forty-six

Cover story

Raw earth is protective enough
to clothe itself with whatever
seeds drift by, sink,
sprout, spread a green
shade of leaves.
Even a bare rock encourages
lichen, and mosses
velvet over the death of trees.
Facts are difficult enough:
like Adam, we soften,
endlessly, our pointed naked souls
with trivialities.

Still, under the new paint
the old clapboards hold on
though we may miss the message
of weathered wood.
The greyed grain and the
warp and the dark knothole
are all true and precious
even if we cringe at a
now and then splinter
in our probing finger.

To the free men of Hungary

We who have been
free men, owners of breath,
careless masters of our bodies,
knowing only one dimension
of the right, the strong, the joyous,
gulping freedom unnoticed with
the good wine of our homeland—
we must learn now
the meaning of bars, and understand
the rhetoric of
mass produced indictment, and intone
the litany of total restriction.
There is a numbing discipline
in undeserved blows
and a new hardness in the voices
we hear. Death
sits with us every day
in the court, in the cell.
And as we raise the cold water
to our mouths
and the hard bread and the dry few
beans, and the dead soup
we are learning a new thanks—
pronouncing a real benediction.
We can tell you more about freedom
now.

III
Inside the Miracle

Getting inside the miracle

No, He is too quick. We never
catch Him at it. He is there
sooner than our thought or prayer.
Searching
backward, we cannot discover *how*
or get inside the miracle.

Even if it were here and now
how would we describe the just-born trees
swimming into place at their green creation,
flowering upward in the air
with all their thin twigs quivering
in the gusts of grace? or the great
white whales fluking
through crystalline seas
like recently-inflated balloons? Who could
time the beat of the man's heart
as the woman comes close enough to fill
his newly-hollow side? Who will
diagram the gynecology
of incarnation, the trigonometry of trinity?
or chemically analyze wine
from a well? or see inside
joints as they loosen, and whole limbs
and lives? Will anyone stand beside
the moving stone? and plot the bright
trajectory of the ascension? and explain
the tongues of fire
telling both heat and light?

Enough. Refrain.
Observe a finished work. Think:
Today—another miracle—the feathered
arrows of my faith may link
God's bow and target.

Spring pond

Look how the sun
lies on the low water!

Spread ripple shaped he
has lost roundness:

Light joined to the pond
in a fluid fusion.

And I, earthy,
wed now to the high Sun

Give God a new shape
to shine in.

Craftsman

Carpenter's son, carpenter's son,
is the wood fine
and smoothly sanded, or rough-grained,
lying along your back? Was it well-planed?
Did they use
a plumbline
when they set you up? Is the angle true?
Why did they choose
that dark, expensive stain
to gloss the timbers
next to your feet and fingers? You
should know— who,
Joseph-trained, judged all trees
for special service.

Carpenter's son, carpenter's son,
were the nails new and cleanly driven
when the dark hammers sang?
Is the earth warped from where you hang,
high enough for a
world view?

Carpenter's son, carpenter's son,
was it a job well done?

parable

riding easily
on the bright
unbroken sea—
bursting with a diversity
of lives—
a remnant salvaged
from a universal debris—
lifted by water above
the world's dark
muddy floor—
washed clean—
expecting the dove
and the sign of green
and light
from an opening door—
God's biggest parable:
the ark

Mustard field

Small flowerhead in this blazing field,
pure lemonpale, poised over your
green gray stalk and leaves under the gray
green afternoon, my husband's camera prepares
itself to tell one kind of truth about you.
Standing near, I have already found my focus—
bright field to yellow patch to single plant
to swaying flower to precise bud.
I see you as God sees me, come
from more than five thousand miles away,
picked, one-in-a-million (was it
chance, choice, destiny?) from the blur of
moving heads in a spring wind.

There is a mustard seed hidden in you.

Now I see you in reverse—retain the detail of
you, a color slide in the mind's eye, enlarge
the vision to a wide-angled view of glory
multiplied from a few seeds.

It is a spring day in Switzerland:
the sun is hidden behind rain, but
light burns up like a promise
from the field, from the mustard flower.

Pneuma

" . . . so it is with the Spirit." John 3:8

The wind breathes where it wishes.
The wind blows where it blows.

A flurry of starlings
scatter like lifted leaves
across the dark October field
driven against
their own warm, southward
impulse; winged instinct
thwarted by
a weight of wind.

The eye of Your storm
sees from the wild height.
Your air augments the world
tearing
away dead wood, testing,
toughening all trees
spreading all seeds
thawing a winter wasteland
sifting the sand, carving
the rock, the water,
in the end
moving the mountain.

Your wind breathes where it wishes,
moves where it wills, sometimes
severs my safe moorings. Sovereign gusts—
buffet my wings with your blowing,
loosen me, lift me to go
wherever you're going.

Prophecy
Genesis 13:16; 22:17

If you can, count the dust, He said,
pointing to the infinities
of diamonds in His sky
and all the silver sands
circling His seven seas.

He might almost as well have said
that Abraham's precious seed
would multiply and spread and shine
like the great golden beach
of dandelion stars, (each soon to send
a dust of seeds with wings
along the shining air)
this spring, in my front yard!

**It is as if infancy
were the whole of incarnation.**

One time of the year
the new-born child
is everywhere,
planted in madonnas' arms
hay mows, stables,
in palaces or farms,
or quaintly, under snowed gables,
gothic angular or baroque plump,
naked or elaborately swathed,
encircled by Della Robbia wreaths,
garnished with whimsical
partridges and pears,
drummers and drums,
lit by oversize stars,
partnered with lambs,
peace doves, sugar plums,
bells, plastic camels in sets of three
as if these were what we need
for eternity.

But Jesus the Man is not to be seen.
We are too wary, these days,
of beards and sandalled feet.

Yet if we celebrate, let it be
that He
has invaded our lives with purpose,
striding over our picturesque traditions,
our shallow sentiment,
overturning our cash registers,
wielding His peace like a sword,
rescuing us into reality,
demanding much more
than the milk and the softness
and the mother warmth

of the baby in the storefront creche,
(only the Man would ask
all, of each of us)
reaching out
always, urgently, with strong
effective love
(only the Man would give
His life and live
again for love of us).

Oh come, let us adore Him—
Christ—*the Lord*.

vision

via dwindling snow and shining
mud, the brown crust gives back
the shimmering of
a spring heat

it is early april
but i see august

moving in the
hot air
above the corn field
(grey husks and stalks
scattered like
bones of an old harvest)
glimpse now the congregation
of bright tassels, the sheaths
swelling with a hundred
hidden kernels, the fluted leaves
flickering
like tongues of green fire

it is a perfect vision
a pentecost of spring

Power failure

By what
anti-miracle have we
lamed the man
who leaped for joy,
lost ninety-nine
sheep,
turned bread
back to stone
and wine
to water?

He who would be great among you

You whose birth broke all the
social & biological rules—
son of the poor who accepted
the worship due a king—
child prodigy debating with
the Temple Th.D.s—you
were the kind who used
a new math
to multiply bread, fish, faith.
You practiced a
radical sociology:
rehabilitated con men &
call girls. You valued women
& other minority groups.
A G.P., you specialized in
heart transplants.
Creator, healer,
shepherd, innovator,
story-teller, weather-maker,
botanist, alchemist,
exorcist, iconoclast,
seeker, seer, motive-sifter,
you were always beyond,
above us. Ahead
of your time, & ours.

And we would like
to be *like* you. Bold
as Boanerges, we hear ourselves
demand: "Admit us
to your avant-garde.
Grant us degree
in all the liberal arts
of heaven."
Why our belligerence?
Why does this whiff of fame

and greatness smell so sweet?
Why must we compete
to be first? Have we forgotten
how you took, simply, cool water
and a towel for our feet?

Stars in apple cores
Matthew 1:9, 10
II Corinthians 4:6
II Peter 1:19

You
are the One who put
stars
in apple cores

God
of all stars and symbols
and all grace,
You have reshaped
the empty space
deep in my apple heart
into a core of light
a star to shine
like Bethlehem's far-
to-near Night Sign:
bright
birth announcement
of Your
Day Star

Poet: silent after Pentecost

I who was thirsty, drank, was satisfied,
became myself a secondary source
of bubbling water—why
was my mouth still dry?

Brushed by dove's feathers
heart and winging mind—
I who had felt flight dared to ask
when will my words fly?

His burning oil from crown
to feet had covered me.
I was a torch for lighting, and for light
yet was my throat still dark.

The overwhelming rush,
the mighty wind wide-spread the blaze.
Yet from my tinder tongue
came not one spark.

Breasting the gusts of praise,
filled with the singing Word
and words, and still
no sound would come.

That Holy Breath, promised,
to teach lungs, larynx, lips
in a needed hour, told mine
until today, "Be dumb!"

Enoch

crossed the gap
another way
he changed his pace
but not
his company

May 20: very early morning

all the field praises Him/all
dandelions are His glory/gold
and silver /all trilliums unfold
white flames above their trinities
of leaves all wild strawberries
and massed wood violets reflect His skies'
clean blue and white
all brambles/all oxeyes
all stalks and stems lift to His light
all young windflower bells
tremble on hair
springs for His air's
carillon touch/last year's yarrow (raising
brittle star skeletons) tells
age is not past praising
all small low unknown
unnamed weeds show His impossible greens
all grasses sing
tone on clear tone
all mosses spread a spring-
soft velvet for His feet
and by all means
all leaves/buds/all flowers cup
jewels of fire and ice
holding up
to His kind morning heat
a silver sacrifice

now
make of our hearts a field
to raise Your praise

. . . for they shall see God.
Matt. 5:8

*"They only saw Jesus—and then but the outside Jesus, or
a little more. They were not pure in heart. . . . They saw
Him with their eyes, but not with those eyes which alone
can see God . . . the thought-eyes, the truth-eyes, the
love-eyes can see Him."—George Macdonald*

Christ risen was rarely recognized by sight.
They had to get beyond the way he looked.
Evidence stronger than his voice and face and footstep
waited to grow in them, to guide their groping
out of despair, their stretching toward belief.

We are as blind as they
until the opening of our deeper eyes
shows *us* the hands that bless and break
our bread, until we finger
wounds that tell *our* healing, or witness
a miracle of fish, dawn-caught
after our long night of empty nets. Handling
his word *we* feel his flesh, his bones, and hear
his voice saying *our* early-morning name.

Angel Vision

Seeing Creation come, they know it well:
the stars, the shoots of green shine for them
one by one. They have eternity to learn
the universe, which once encompassing, angels
forget not. Clean as steel wires, shining
as frost, making holiness beautiful, aiming
at the Will of God like arrows flaming
to a target, earthy solidity presents no
barrier to their going. Easily they slope
through the rind of the world, the atoms
pinging in their celestial orifices. Matter
& anti-matter open before them like a bible.
Inhabiting the purposes of God, Who is
the Lord of all their Hosts, in Deep Space
their congregation wages war with swords of fire
& power & great joy, seizing from the
Hierarchies of Darkness Andromeda's boundaries
& all constellations. The rising Day Star
is their standard bearer, as on earth they stay
the Adversary's slaughter of the Sons of God.
                                        Praise
is their delight also. Rank on rank they sing
circularly around the Throne, dancing together
in a glory, clapping hands at all rebellion
repented of, or sheep returned. They who
accompany the bright spiriting up of a redeemed
swimmer from the final wave, who trace
the grey, heavy clot that marks the drowning
of the profane to his own place—how can we
think to escape their fiery ministry? We listen
for their feathers, miss the shaft of light
at our shoulder. We tread our gauntlet paths
unknowing, covered by shields of angels. (The ass
sees one & shames us for blindness.) "Fear not"s
unfurl like banners over their appearing, yet
we tremble at their faces.

Seraphim sing
in no time zone. Cherubim see as clearly on
as back, invest acacia planks with arkhood in
their certainty (whose winged ornamenting gilds
the tabernacle shade.) Comprehending the
compacted plan centered in every seed, the grown
plant is no more real to them & no surprise.
Dampened by neither doubt nor supposition,
they understand what happens to a worm. And if
we ask—Did he please God? Did he fulfill
the Eternal Plan for worms, drilling the soil,
digesting it? & his strange hermaphroditic
replication—did he do it well? & what will
happen to his wormy spirit when he shrivels back
to soil? heavenly Beings answer instantly,
giving God high praise for faithful worms.
The archangel sees with eyes quicker than ours &
unconfused by multiplicity. For him, reality's
random choice is all clear cause & effect:
each star of snow tells of intelligence; each
cell carries its own code; at a glance he knows
from whence the crests of all the wrinkles on
the sea rebound. He has eternity to tell
it all, & to rejoice.

But what is this
conjunction of straw & splendor? The echo of
sharp laughter from a crowd (of men bent from
the image of the firstmade man) as nails
pierce flesh, pierces the Bright Ones with
perplexity. They see the Maker's hands helpless
against Made Wood. The bond is sealed with
God's blood. Thus is Love's substance darkness
to their light. The Third Day sweetens the deep
Riddle. Heralds now of a new Rising, they have
eternity to solve it, & to praise.

Notes on the poems

Behind the walls
As our family drove past this new home under construction Sunday by
Sunday on our way to church, the contrast between the wooden uprights of
the shell (the "secret trees") and the living trees on the lot surrounding
it insisted on being written into a poem.

To a Christmas two-year-old
The concept of the substitutionary death of Christ "in our room and stead"
takes on a new meaning when we realize who died as substitutes for him.

The Groundhog
The "doubtful fable" mentioned in the fifth line is just that—an invention
to lend a spurious validity to the Christmas greeting I was writing around
the small person of a hedgehog in an early German woodcut reproduced
by the New York Metropolitan Museum of Art as one of its 1972 Christmas cards.

To Clyde S. Kilby
The subject of this poem, a close and dear friend, has for a number of
years been the moving force behind the collection of manuscripts, letters,
photographs, first editions and other memorabilia of C. S. Lewis,
George MacDonald, Dorothy Sayers, J. R. R. Tolkien, Charles
Williams (and other writers) which are housed in the Marion E.
Wade Collection at Wheaton College.

Poem finding a path
A partial explanation of why it is easier to *write* poetry than
to *speak* poetically!

O'Hareport: Taking off
Metaphor being what it is—an effort to see an old view from a
new angle—the perspective available from a plane window seems
made to order for the poet.

Shooting gallery
There seems to me to be an analogy between shallow praying
and the artificiality of an amusement arcade shooting gallery,
with its pop guns and wooden ducks, which shows up real
prayer (and real hunting) in sharp relief.

The tenacity of memory
All the senses are at work successively in this poem about the
reality of remembered images.

The Joining
Substitution and co-inherence are concepts implicit both in
Paul's epistles and in the writings of Charles Williams. I began this
poem after reading the article by Cheryl Forbes on Charles Williams' work
and thought in *Christianity Today*, Aug. 29, 1975.

Anatomy of the Invisible
In her book *Hidden Art*, Edith Schaeffer writes of God, the
Artist, who created "*All* things! Visible. . . . *All* things! Invisible!
The things I know are there but cannot see—wind and gravity,
atoms and electrons, oxygen and sound waves." Our mind's
eye questions: "In what forms do these invisible realities exist?"

Cover story
This poem grew from the sight of a fallen, rotting tree trunk
near InterVarsity's Cedar Campus, in Upper Michigan. The dead
wood was made beautiful by the mosses and lichens which
clothed its decay.

Getting Inside the Miracle
Having both seen and experienced instantaneous divine healing,
curiosity urges me to focus a microscope lens on the bone cells
in some calcified joint which is suddenly returned to mobility
in answer to prayer. I want to see *how* it happens, *when* it happens!
But the mystery of miracle remains because "He is too quick.
We never catch him at it."

Spring Pond
Passing a pool of melted snow by the roadside as we were
driving to town, my three year-old Kristin saw the sun's reflection
in the water shattered by a quick breeze and cried out, "The
sun's not round any more!" At the next stop light on Gary Avenue
this poem was scribbled on the back of a grocery list.

Prophecy
To any lawn tender, the profusion of spring dandelions must
seem comparable to the sand of the sea, the stars in the sky
and the desert dust to which God likened Abraham's future
descendents for numbers!

Poet: Silent after Pentecost
After a life-changing experience with God the Holy Spirit in 1972,
the flow of poems was cut off in my life. It was as if my mind
had changed gears, and poetry was, for a time, a non-essential.
After a while I began to wonder whether my use of a "heavenly
language" meant the loss of expression in the earthly one.
With this poem came the answer, and I knew what Isaiah meant
when he prophesied that "the tongue of the dumb shall sing."

. . . for they shall see God.
This poem does not minimize the importance of the physical,
bodily resurrection of Christ. It does emphasize our individual need
of a personal, inner revelation of Jesus risen *for us*.